W9-AOR-223

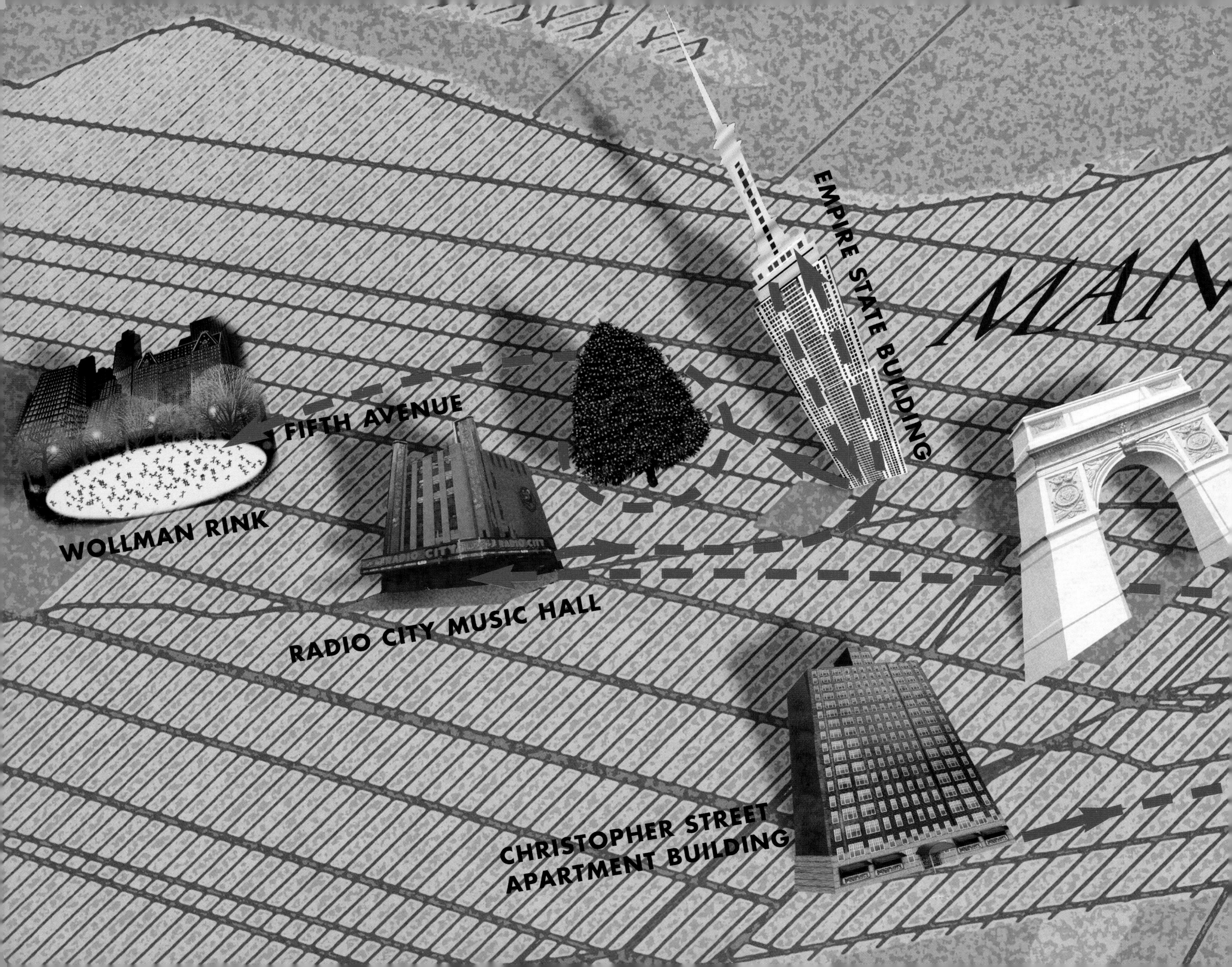
EMPIRE STATE BUILDING
FIFTH AVENUE
WOLLMAN RINK
RADIO CITY MUSIC HALL
CHRISTOPHER STREET
APARTMENT BUILDING

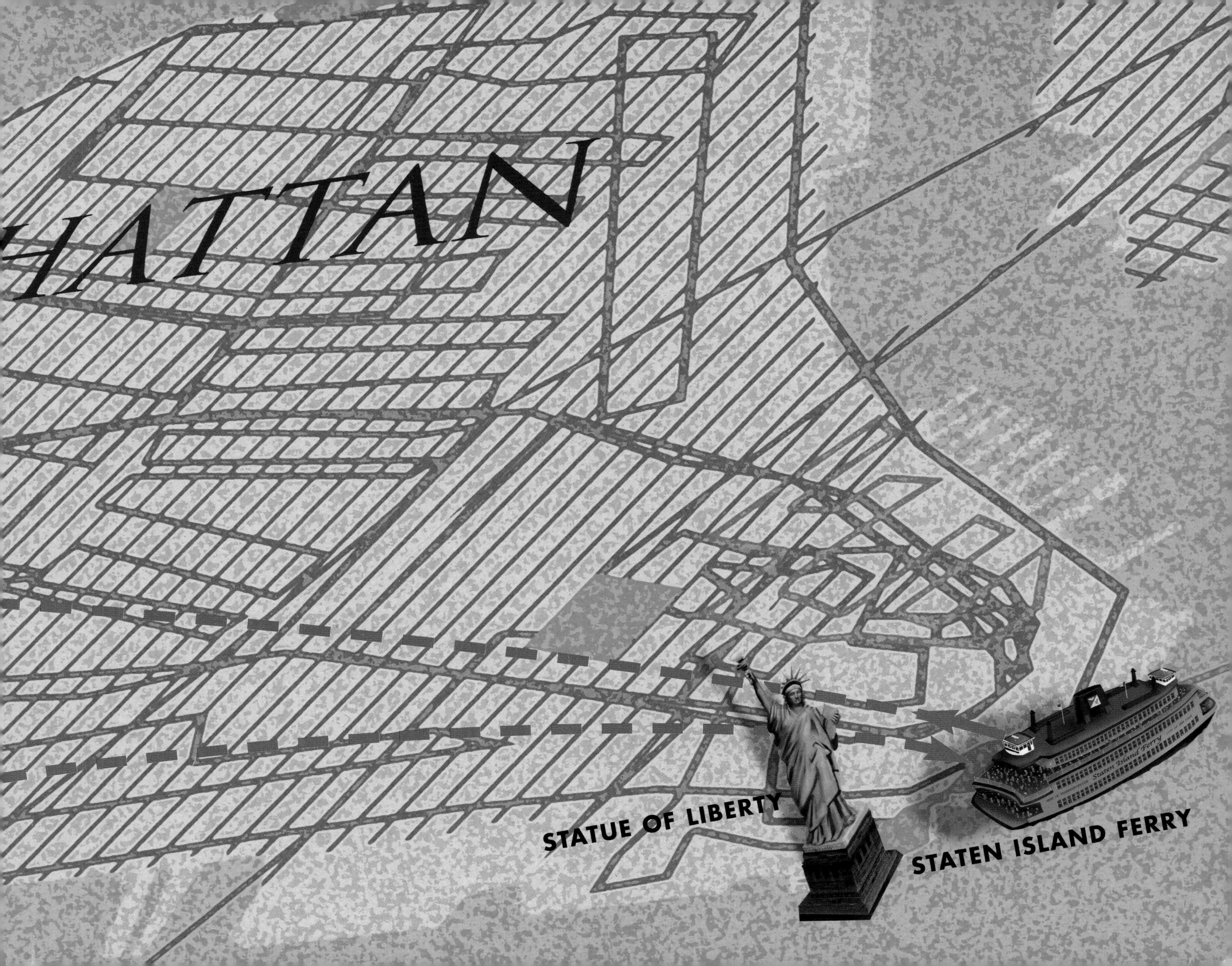
HATTAN
STATUE OF LIBERTY
STATEN ISLAND FERRY
Staten Island Ferry

POOCH on the LOOSE

A CHRISTMAS ADVENTURE

by STEVEN KROLL

illustrated by MICHAEL GARLAND

Marshall Cavendish Children

Text copyright © 2005 by Steven Kroll
Illustrations copyright © 2005 by Michael Garland
All rights reserved

Marshall Cavendish, 99 White Plains Road, Tarrytown, NY 10591
www.marshallcavendish.us/kids

LIBRARY OF CONGRESS CATALOGING-IN-PUBLICATION DATA
Kroll, Steven.
Pooch on the loose : a Christmas adventure / by Steven Kroll ; illustrated by Michael Garland.
p. cm.
Summary: Bart, an adventurous dog, escapes from his master one day and takes a whirlwind tour of New York City to enjoy all the Christmas sights.
ISBN: 978-0-7614-5443-4 (paperback) ISBN: 0-7614-5239-7 (hardcover)
[1. Dogs—Fiction. 2. Christmas—Fiction. 3. New York (N.Y.)—Fiction.] I. Garland, Michael, 1952– ill. II. Title.
PZ7.K9225Po 2005
[E]—dc22
2004027510

The illustrations are rendered in Photoshop.
Book design by Michael Nelson

First Marshall Cavendish paperback edition, 2008
Printed in Malaysia
First edition
1 3 5 6 4 2

To Kathleen, my New York City girl

—S. K.

To Peggy

—M. G.

Bart's my name.

I'm a New York City dog.

I live in a big apartment building
in Greenwich Village
with my owner, Max.

79

I am very good to him.
No doubt about it.
I smother him with doggy kisses.
I heel when we go for our long walks in Washington Square Park.

The other dogs in my building think I've got it made,
but even though Max is special, I'm not so sure.
I'm always on a leash when we go for walks.
The only time I get to ride in a taxi is to the vet.
I'd like to do the town, see the sights, especially at Christmas.

One December morning, Max comes home with a Christmas tree.
When he opens the door, I get my chance.
I scamper down the stairs.
I'm outta here!
Time to have fun.
Where should I go first?

The Staten Island Ferry!
Max has never taken me.
He says it makes him seasick.
I race to the Christopher Street subway station.
I dash under the turnstile and jump onto a train.
Whoopee!
I leap onto a seat.
People look every which way,
pretending not to notice.

116 St
110 St
103 St

DEPT OF TRANSPORTATION
Staten Island Ferry
CITY OF NEW YORK

At the last stop, I dash through the door
and scurry up the stairs to the ferry terminal.
Lucky me. A ferry has just arrived.
I find a seat on deck. Oh, the crisp cold air!
It makes my whiskers twitch.
I can see the harbor.
I can see the Statue of Liberty!
Wow! I stand on my hind legs, the Dog of Liberty,
the dog who is glad to be free.

But I have to do something
that feels more like Christmas.
I know what it's gotta be.

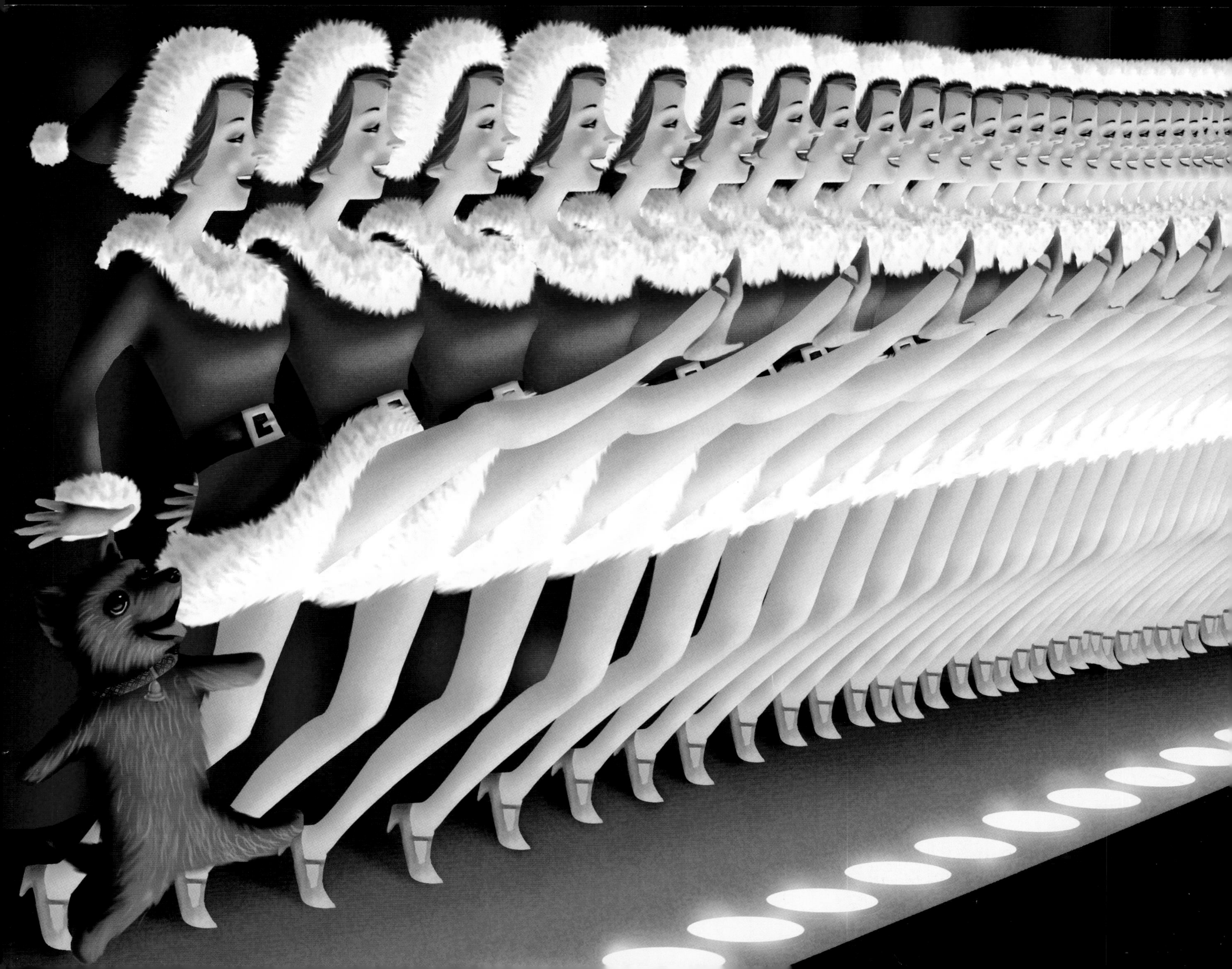

I take the ferry back to Manhattan,
then the subway uptown to Radio City Music Hall.
I trot into the theater past a lot of kids in fancy Christmas clothes.
The curtain rises. Oh, boy!
There are the Rockettes!
I *have* to dance with them.
Barking loudly, I jump onto the stage.
One, two, three, kick.
I don't need to tell you what happens next.
People in uniforms try to grab me.
One of them is a cop!

I take off and head for the Empire State Building.
The elevators are packed like boxes of dog biscuits.
All these holiday humans in their smelly boots.
Finally, I get to the observation deck.
Wow! What a view!
The buildings are lit up like Christmas trees.
If only Max could see me here.

I see Central Park.
I've always wanted to go ice-skating at the Wollman Rink.
No time like the present!

SALE
MERRY CHRISTMAS
SALE
TAXI FARE

I ride the elevators down to the street and run up Fifth Avenue.
I scoot past the Christmas windows at Saks and Lord & Taylor.
I'm a pooch on the loose.

I run by Rockefeller Center.
I am so hungry, I grab a pretzel right out of the hand of a French tourist.
Ooh-la-la! What a treat!

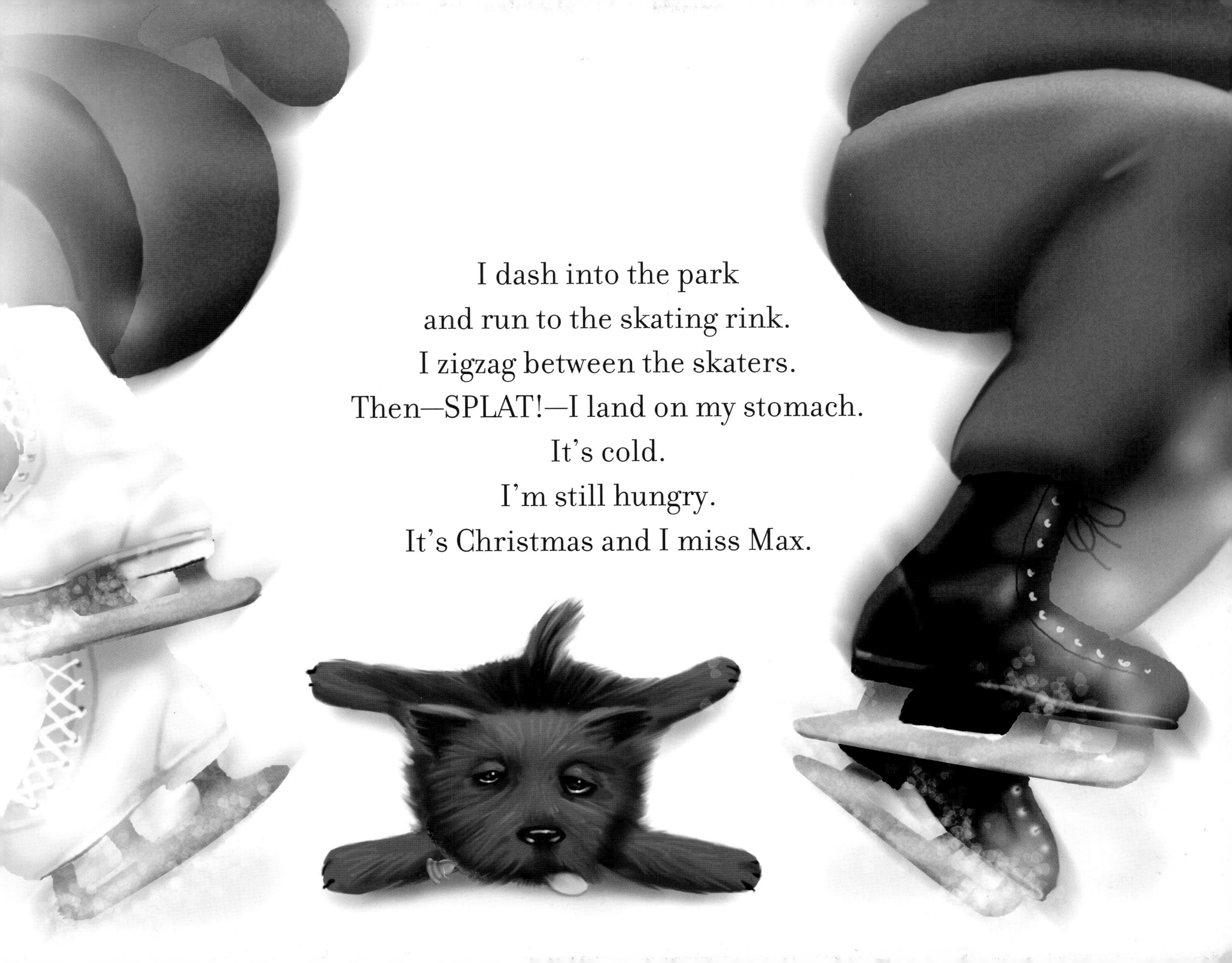

I dash into the park
and run to the skating rink.
I zigzag between the skaters.
Then—SPLAT!—I land on my stomach.
It's cold.
I'm still hungry.
It's Christmas and I miss Max.

Where is Max, anyway?
He's home!
At least I hope he is.
I have to go find him.
I slip and slide to the edge of the rink.
I run though the park and head for the Village.

79

I sneak back into our building.
This time I take the elevator.
I scratch on our door.
Hurry up, Max.
It's dinnertime.

Max opens the door and scoops me into his arms.
"Bart," he cries, "you're home! I've been worried sick."
"Arf, arf," I bark.
Freedom is good, but Max is BEST!

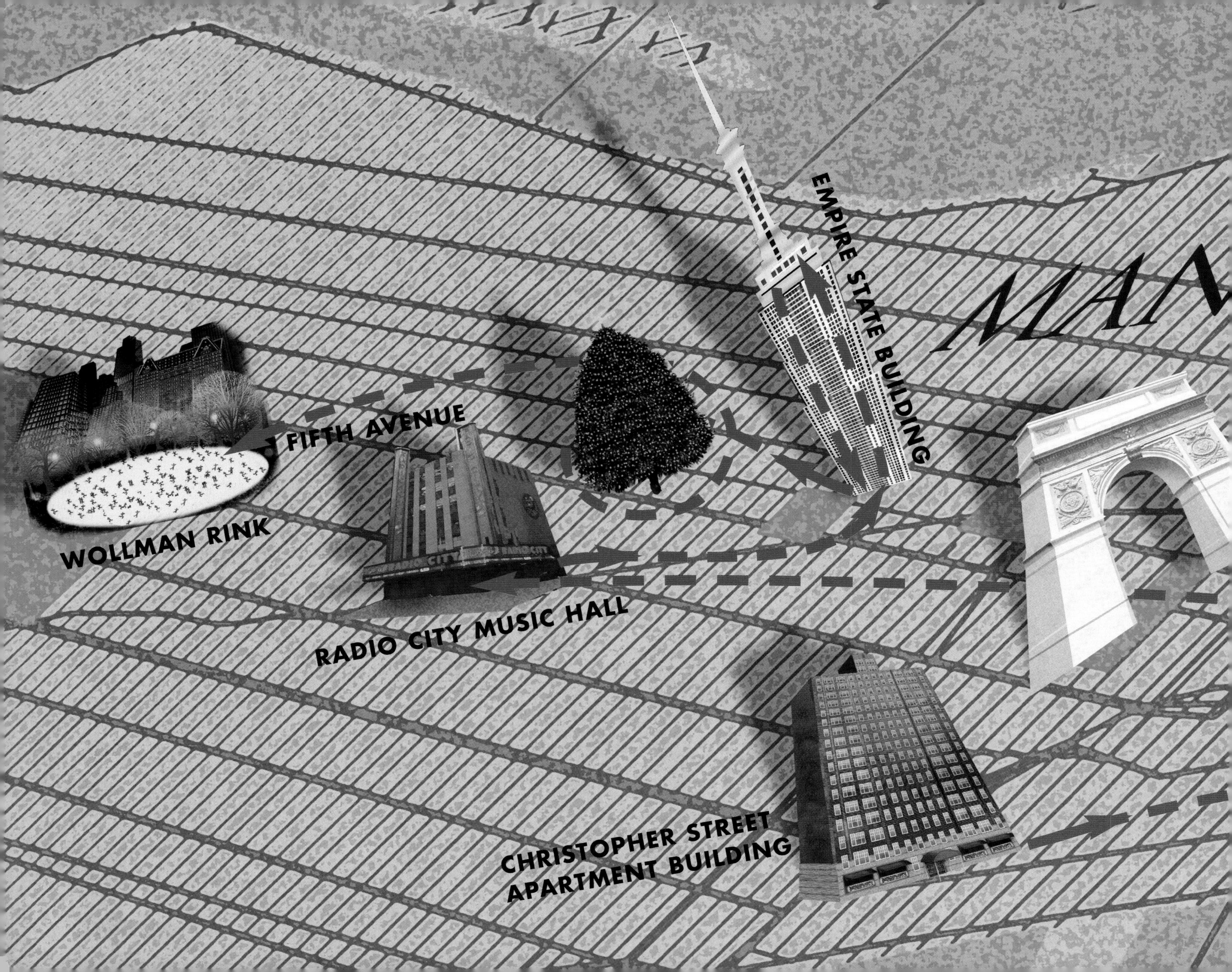
FIFTH AVENUE
WOLLMAN RINK
RADIO CITY MUSIC HALL
EMPIRE STATE BUILDING
CHRISTOPHER STREET
APARTMENT BUILDING

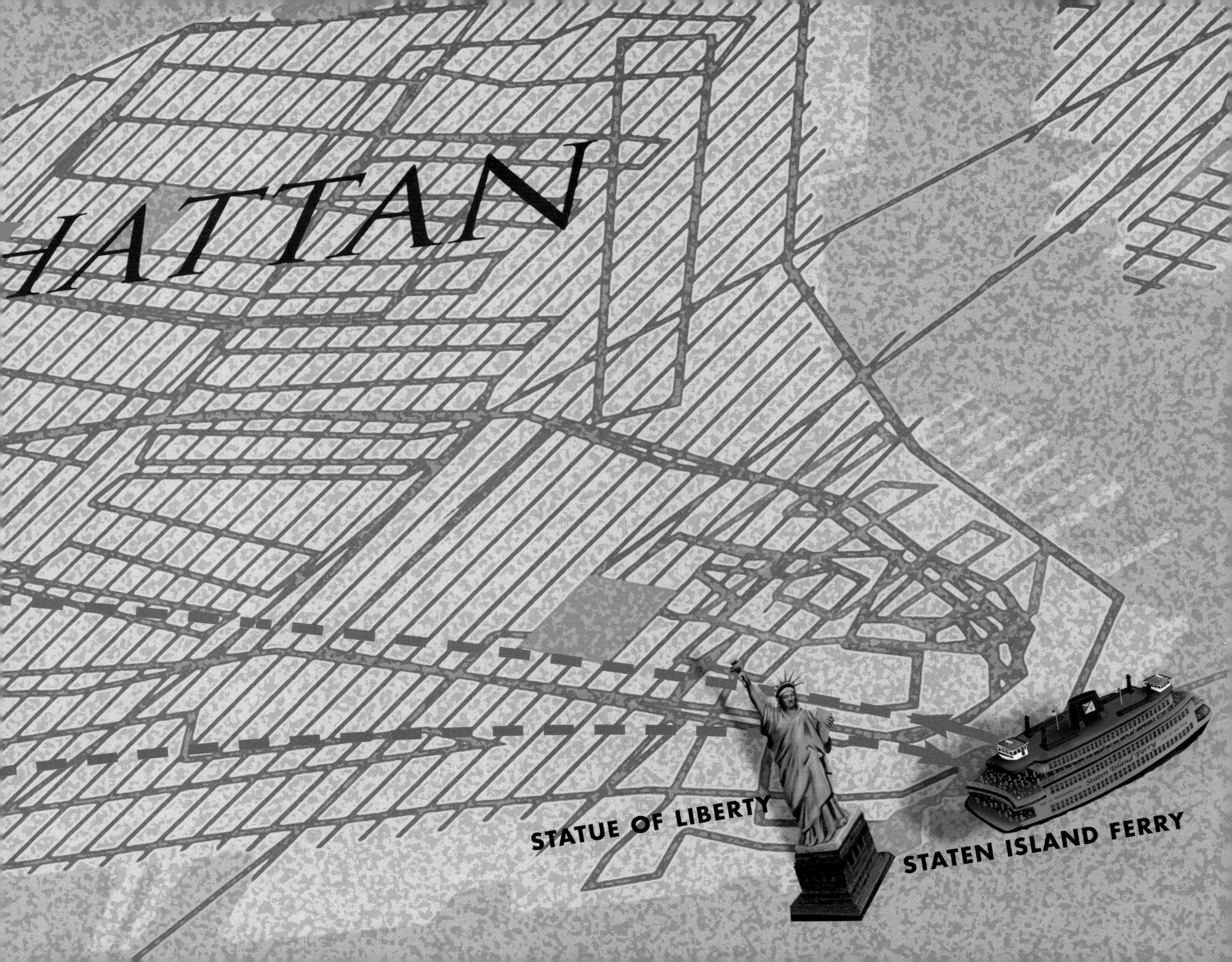

ATTAN
STATUE OF LIBERTY
STATEN ISLAND FERRY